AuthorHouse™
1663 Liberty Drive
Bloomington, IN 47403
www.authorhouse.com
Phone: 1-800-839-8640

First published by AuthorHouse 09/01/2011

ISBN: 978-1-4567-8823-0 (sc)

Printed in the United States of America

Any people depicted in stock imagery provided by Thinkstock are models,
and such images are being used for illustrative purposes only.
Certain stock imagery © Thinkstock.

This book is printed on acid-free paper.

Because of the dynamic nature of the Internet, any web addresses or links contained in this book may have changed
since publication and may no longer be valid. The views expressed in this work are solely those of the author and do not
necessarily reflect the views of the publisher, and the publisher hereby disclaims any responsibility for them.

authorHOUSE®

Princesses and Dinosaurs

By Kimberly Wasserman Hayes

Illustrated by Whitney Orr

I put on my pink princess dress and glittery crown.

I grab my sword and with a big roar,
scare the dinosaur out of town.

ROAR!

I dance and sway to a pretty sound.

I carry wriggly worms that I find on the ground.

With my best dress on,
I am the belle of the ball.

With my tool box near, I fix the crack in the wall.

Oh yuck! I fell in the messy sand.

Oh Daddy, Daddy, put the slimy fish in my hand.

I want to be a ballerina. See me twirl on my toes.

I want to be a doctor. Let me look up your nose.

I draw hearts and rainbows for my grandmas far away.

I play king of the mountain and shout, "Save the day!"

I pet the fluffy puppy, as he wags his tail.

Mommy doesn't like it, when I kiss a snail.

I love my brother, so I give him a big hug.

I push my brother, so I can get the bug.

Wow! pink flowers for my auntie's locket.

Wow! Cool rocks for my pocket.

No! I must wear the pink dress with the shoes that are shiny.

Yes! I will step in every puddle and get very muddy.

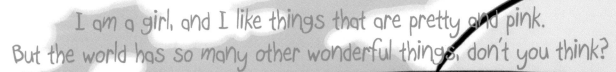

I am a girl, and I like things that are pretty and pink.
But the world has so many other wonderful things, don't you think?

24

CPSIA information can be obtained
at www.ICGtesting.com
Printed in the USA
LVIC060323030919
629753LV00001B/11